Murder in the Tides

A Little Firling Mystery – Book Eight

by Belinda Chavremootoo

Dedication

For every cat who ever solved a mystery quietly before the humans caught up. Specially one.

Text Copyright

© 2025 Belinda Chavremootoo

All rights reserved.

This is a work of fiction. Names, characters, places, and incidents are the product of the author's imagination or are used fictitiously. Any resemblance to actual persons, living or dead, businesses, locales, or events is purely coincidental.

No part of this book may be reproduced, stored in a retrieval system, or transmitted in any form or by any means—electronic, mechanical, photocopying, recording, or otherwise—without express written permission of the copyright owner.

First Edition

Coming Soon: Murder in the Quiet Hours

A Little Firling Mystery – Book Nine

In the village of Little Firling, quiet is a comfort. A rhythm. A way of life.

But when a string of peaceful hospital deaths begins to echo with unease, retired professor Annabel Lennox Deighton starts to wonder if silence has become a mask... for murder.

As whispers emerge, so do names once thought forgotten — including someone Evie loved and lost. This time, the mystery isn't about what was taken. It's about what was never questioned.

Because the most dangerous killer may not hide in shadows — but in plain sight.

And the most terrifying thing of all?

No one thought to look.

Table of Contents

Prologue

Then

She didn't want to go.

She stood at the edge of the pool, shoes still on, arms folded tight across her chest. The villa was too quiet. Too clean. It didn't feel like a meeting — it felt like a trap dressed in white cushions and glass walls.

She had taken a photo. Quickly. Quietly.

Just in case.

If I don't come back...

She didn't finish the message. She didn't get the chance.

The last thing she heard was the water.

And then nothing at all.

Chapter 1

The roses had bloomed too early. The delphiniums were already drooping. Even the dahlias looked exhausted.

Annabel couldn't blame them.

The heat had settled over Little Firling like a sleepy cat — heavy, uninterested in moving, and entirely unimpressed with the idea of productivity. No one in the Hare & Hound was talking about much else, except how the weather had effectively ended gardening season three weeks too early.

"You can't even garden in it," said Gillian at the next table, fanning herself with a laminated menu.

"Just watering and glaring at the sun like it's personally offended you."

"I was up at six," chimed in Marjorie, "trying to beat the heat. Gave up after twenty minutes. The carrots looked like they'd gone on strike."

Laughter rippled around the pub. Bernard, leaning against the bar with an ice cube melting on his neck, declared, "If this keeps up, I'll start serving soup chilled and calling it a new trend."

* * *

Annabel stirred her lemonade with theatrical resignation.

Evie sat opposite her, barefoot in sandals and radiating satisfaction, toes curled under the table like a smug fox.

"It's too hot to be serious," Evie said. "Which is why I have made a booking that is deeply unserious for us."

Annabel narrowed her eyes. "Does it involve questionable fruit-based cocktails?"

"No, but now I wish it did. Boat tour."

"Pardon?"

"Little Firling's got one now," Evie said cheerfully. "Starts right down at the old mill dock. Doesn't require so much as a toe in the sea — unless you fall in, which would be very entertaining."

Annabel arched an eyebrow. "Since when do we have a dock, let alone a boat tour?"

"Since someone clever figured out tourists will pay twenty pounds to look at rocks from the other side."

At the far end of the room, someone muttered that it was "a bit indulgent for a place like this." Another replied, "Well, it's nicer than the duck pond, and you don't have to leave town."

✳✳✳

Beneath the table, Persephone let out a soft, judgmental chuff and swatted lightly at Evie's swinging foot.

Evie looked down. "I told you she heard the word 'boat.'"

Annabel sighed. "She'll never forgive us."

"That's fine," Evie said. "We'll bribe her with tuna and sunbeams."

Annabel sipped her lemonade and stared into the middle distance, where the ceiling fan whirred like a dying dragonfly. Heat shimmered outside the window, warping the view of Bernard's prize hanging baskets into a mirage of overwatered petunias.

"Fine," she said. "I'll come. But if I get sunburned, I'll hold you personally responsible."

"Good. I've prepared a speech and everything."

***

They finished their drinks in silence.

Outside, the air rippled like it was trying to hide something just beneath the surface.

Chapter 2

Persephone made it known from the moment they left the cottage that she considered the entire endeavour beneath her.

She did not care for the leash.

She did not care for the sun.

She most certainly did not care for the idea of a floating platform held together with rope and optimism.

She meowed once — low, sharp, and with the distinct tone of legal objection — as Annabel gently lifted her onto the dock.

"Oh, stop it," Annabel muttered. "It's a short ride, and you're not going overboard. You're on a leash. You'll be fine."

Persephone did not dignify that with a response. She simply crouched low, tail twitching, and emitted a noise that sounded like it came from a much larger predator.

***

Evie was already chatting with the tour guide — a sun-wrinkled woman in her fifties named Jen who wore polarized sunglasses and had a voice like laughter and salt.

"You brought your cat?" she asked cheerfully.

"She refused to be left behind," Annabel said smoothly, as if Persephone had packed her own overnight bag.

Jen grinned. "Haven't had that before. You'll have the most interesting passenger list of the week."

***

The boat was a tidy thing — white fiberglass, bright blue trim, cushioned benches around the edge, and a small shaded area near the console. Life jackets were optional, drinks were available in a cooler, and there was a tiny laminated map no one looked at.

The dock creaked gently as they boarded. A few other passengers joined them — a young couple already taking selfies, an older man with binoculars, and a woman in a floppy sunhat who immediately pulled out a novel.

Persephone settled by Annabel's feet, hating everything.

"She's sulking," Evie whispered.

"She's planning," Annabel corrected. "Revenge, probably."

***

They set off just after ten. The water shimmered under the hull, clear and inviting, the coastline rippling with wildflowers and gulls. Jen kept up a steady stream of commentary — caves formed by centuries of erosion, seabirds nesting in impossible crags, tales of smugglers and storms.

Annabel let the sun warm her shoulders and tried to relax.

But just as they rounded the bend toward a quiet inlet, her gaze caught on a cove ahead — one they hadn't seen before. Tucked between two narrow cliffs. Still. Empty.

And somehow... waiting.

Chapter 3

The boat had gone quiet.

Not completely — Jen was still chatting about sea arches and nesting gulls — but something in the air shifted. The kind of quiet that doesn't mean *nothing is happening,* but that *something is about to.*

Persephone felt it first.

She rose from her position at Annabel's feet and sniffed the air, slow and sharp, her nose twitching once. Then again.

She turned her head toward the cliffs — the cove just coming into view, hidden behind jagged rock and sun glare.

"What is it?" Annabel murmured, watching her.

Persephone didn't answer, of course. She just stared. Still. Tense.

Then came the sound — so faint only *she* could hear it.

A soft, high vibration. Not a bird. Not a boat.

Something in the water? Or... *beneath it?*

She stood fully, tail low, ears forward — and hissed.

A short, sharp, surgical warning.

***

Evie looked down. "That's not her dramatic hiss. That's her *something's wrong* hiss."

Annabel followed her gaze toward the cove.

The sunlight was just hitting the water right — golden, still, sparkling like glass. Too still.

"Jen," Annabel called to the front. "Could we slow down a moment?"

The guide nodded and adjusted the throttle, easy, no fuss.

Everyone leaned toward the cliffs, admiring the view.

Only Annabel leaned the other way — toward the waterline just ahead. Toward something pale.

Something... *soft.*

***

The ripples moved oddly.

Annabel stepped toward the edge of the boat.

And that's when she saw it.

A dress.

Hair.

Skin so pale it looked like light itself.

***

Behind her, Persephone growled — low, guttural, from somewhere deeper than her throat.

Evie stepped back, hand flying to her mouth.

Annabel didn't look away.

"There's someone in the water."

Chapter 4

There was a moment — after Jen cut the engine, after the boat rocked to stillness, after Annabel spoke — when no one said a word.

The kind of silence that arrives *after* a name is forgotten, *before* a truth is spoken.

The girl floated just beneath the surface, hair fanning out around her like kelp. A pale summer dress clung to her limbs. One arm was caught in a curl of seaweed.

She looked... still.

"She must've drowned," someone whispered behind Annabel.

And just like that, the silence broke.

"Poor thing. Probably swam out alone."

"You can get caught in a current without even realizing it."

"Didn't we have a red flag warning last week?"

The woman in the floppy sunhat folded her book and muttered, "Kids these days think they're invincible."

***

Annabel knelt at the edge of the boat and studied the girl.

No shoes.

No bag.

No watch or phone.

And strangely — *no visible injuries.* Not a scratch from the rocks. Not a bruise.

Persephone hadn't moved. She was sitting up now, ears back, body taut. Watching the girl like she might move.

Evie stood next to her, one hand over her mouth, the other gripping the side of the boat.

"Annabel?" she asked, quietly. "Do you think... it's what they said?"

Annabel didn't answer.

Because the girl didn't have a panicked expression on her face.

She didn't look like someone who had fought.

She didn't even look like she had jumped.

She looked like someone who had *been placed.*

***

The guide, Jen, radioed the coastguard with the calm of someone who'd done this before — once or twice too many times.

"Unresponsive body. Female. Early twenties, we think. No sign of life. No visible injuries."

Annabel's eyes never left the girl.

"She doesn't look like she came here alone," she said softly.

Evie blinked. "What?"

"You don't come coasteering in a summer dress. Not without shoes. Not without a bag. Not to this cove. Not without being seen."

***

The woman in the sunhat nodded, almost relieved.

"Maybe it was suicide, then."

Another voice jumped in. "Oh yes. That makes sense. She looks... peaceful. Doesn't she?"

Everyone nodded a little too quickly.

Because *suicide is easier.*

It ends the conversation.

Murder doesn't.

***

Evie whispered, "Could she have drifted in? From further up the coast?"

Annabel didn't answer right away.

She glanced at the rocks flanking the cove. Jagged. Close. Shallow water.

"It's possible," she said finally. "If the current was right."

A pause.

"But she doesn't have the scrapes you'd expect if she passed through those rocks."

She stood slowly.

"I'm not saying how she got here."

"I'm just saying… she doesn't look like

she got here by accident."

Chapter 5

The coastguard's boat arrived with the low hum of authority — cutting cleanly across the water, a blue light flickering against the cliffs like a silent alarm.

No one on the tour boat spoke as it pulled alongside.

Jen waved them over and gave a quick report. Her voice had lost its cheer. Now she just sounded tired.

"Young woman. No signs of life. No ID."

****

A female officer in mirrored sunglasses stepped aboard first. Mid-forties. Calm. Clipboard in hand, but her eyes never stopped moving.

"We'll take it from here," she said. "Everyone, please stay where you are."

Someone on the bench whispered, "Are we witnesses now?"

"You were here when she was found," the officer replied. "That makes you important. Please don't leave."

***

Evie sat next to Annabel, face pale. Persephone had retreated under the bench again, curled tight, tail twitching. Still alert.

Annabel watched the coastguard team work — gloves, photos, measurements. Everything by the book.

"No visible trauma," the officer muttered to her partner. "Doesn't look like a fall. Clothes intact."

The girl was lifted gently from the water. Her arm slipped from the seaweed. Her hand hung limp.

"We'll transport her to the coroner's office. Full post-mortem," the officer said aloud. "We'll need everyone's names and contact details before disembarking."

***

PC Tom Oakes appeared with a clipboard and a printed passenger manifest. He looked a little seasick and entirely overwhelmed.

"If everyone could please confirm their name against the list..."

One by one, people complied. Grumbling, but compliant. Names ticked off. Details noted.

****

Until Annabel glanced toward the far bench.

"Wasn't there a woman with a red scarf?"

Evie frowned. "Yes. She had the big sunhat."

Annabel turned to the officer. "You're missing a passenger."

PC Oakes checked the list. "We had eleven. Only ten here."

"She's gone," Annabel said quietly.

***

The clipboard froze in mid-air.

"No one's left the boat," the officer said.

"Not from here," Annabel replied. "But maybe before you got here."

She looked out across the dock.

No sign of her.

Just a half-empty water bottle on the bench.

And a lipstick-stained takeaway coffee cup.

Chapter 6

It was early. Too early for tea, but Annabel poured a cup anyway.

Outside the kitchen window, the dahlias looked less smug than usual — finally cowed by the heat. Even the bees were sluggish this morning. The world felt suspended, like the air had thickened just enough to hold everything in place.

She sat at the table with her notebook, the one she didn't call a case journal — but used like one.

On the top page:

No ID

No injuries (external)

No bag.

No shoes.

No bruises.

No witness.

No name.

She'd underlined that last one twice.

***

Annabel had just opened her second notebook when the call came.

She didn't jump, but she felt it — that small tightening in her spine. Like something shifting, slightly, before it fell.

She wasn't expecting it — not today, not this early. But when she saw the coroner's number on the screen, she answered without hesitation.

"Dr. Jameson."

"Professor Deighton," he said.

"You left me a message wanting to know more about the body found in the water. You've... been involved in a few cases now. More than a few, if I recall correctly."

Annabel raised an eyebrow, though no one could see it.

"That's one way to put it."

A pause on the line.

"You might be interested to know," Jameson continued, "that it looks like we have another one."

"Murder?" she asked, quietly.

"I didn't say that," he replied. "But...
the case is no longer being considered
accidental."

***

Annabel moved to her kitchen table;
notebook already open. Persephone
glanced up from the floor but didn't
bother standing.

"What changed?" Annabel asked.

"At first, nothing did. No injuries. No
drugs. No ID. Just drowning."

"But?"

"We re-examined the body after two
days. Some bruising emerged — faint,

along the upper back. Like someone held her down."

Jameson's voice lowered slightly.

"We tested the water. You'd be surprised how often bodies drift."

"And?"

"Not seawater. Not from the cove. Not even the river."

Another pause.

"The water in her lungs is chlorinated. Treated. Synthetic profile. No marine diatoms."

"A swimming pool," Annabel said.

"We're treating it as a suspicious death."

He didn't say murder.

He didn't need to.

***

When the call ended, Annabel sat still for a moment, letting the quiet return.

Then she picked up her pen and underlined a note she'd already written hours ago:

No name. No shoes. No reason.

And beneath that, in her usual neat script:

Wrong water. Wrong place. Wrong story.

She glanced at Persephone, now grooming a paw like nothing had happened.

"Shall we go find a pool?" she said softly.

Persephone didn't answer.

But her tail flicked once — a slow yes.

Chapter 7

The air was already thick with heat by the time Annabel stepped into the Hare & Hound. Inside, the fans wheezed gently and the conversation was slower than usual — everyone too warm for theatrics, too curious not to talk.

Someone had left a copy of the *Firling Gazette* on the bar, folded twice, damp from someone's elbow.

"Shame about the girl," a voice muttered from the corner booth. "Drifted in like a bit of seaweed."

"Young, wasn't she?" replied another. "They said she looked peaceful. Like she just stopped swimming."

"Probably one of those tourists who think cliffs are romantic."

***

Bernard caught Annabel's eye as she approached the counter.

"You here for lemonade or loose ends?" he asked, polishing a glass.

"A bit of both," she said. "You know how it goes."

***

She didn't press — not yet.

Just asked gently, in the way people answer without realizing they're doing it.

"Anyone in lately asking about a rental? A job? Seemed a bit... out of place?"

Most of the answers were vague.

"Could've been one of the summer girls. They always come and go, don't they?"

"There was one staying near Rosehill a year or so ago. Quiet. Could be the same girl. Or not."

"Might've seen someone like her on the path to the post office, but you know... they all blur together."

* * *

At the bakery, Mira Harrington shook her head.

"She doesn't sound local. Maybe from one of the estates? But they've got new people every season."

Nathan, the groundskeeper, was trimming the hedge outside the church when Annabel passed.

"Funny you ask," he said, pausing. "I do remember a girl. Last summer, maybe the one before. Walked past the church a few times. Looked... not lost exactly. But like she didn't want to be seen."

"Do you remember her face?"

He frowned. "Not really. Thin. Dark hair, I think. But maybe that's just what I expect now."

***

By the end of the day, Annabel had three pages of near-memories, of could-be, and of not-sure.

No one remembered her.

Not clearly.

Not enough to be useful.

Not yet.

***

Back at Honeystone Cottage, she poured herself a glass of water and sat beside Persephone, who was curled in a patch of shade with an expression of long-suffering disdain.

Evie came in holding a shopping bag and dropped it on the counter.

"Any progress?"

"Only that everyone's convinced they've seen someone like her... but no one's sure if it's actually her."

Evie sighed. "People want a story, not a memory."

Annabel nodded slowly. "That's the problem. *She's not a story yet. Just a shape* in the water."

Chapter 8

The photo was small.

Top right corner of page three, just under the council's bin collection schedule and beside a recipe for elderflower cordial.

The *Firling Gazette* didn't do "breaking news." But it knew how to plant a headline just quiet enough to be read *by everyone*.

"Police Appeal: Young Woman Found in Water – Can You Identify Her?"

Annabel stared at the image — a cropped, cleaned-up headshot from the coroner's file. The girl's eyes were closed.

Her expression soft. But the line of her cheekbone, the wave of her hair — unmistakable.

Now *she was real.*

***

Evie dropped the paper on the kitchen table.

"So now the village gets a face. And everyone suddenly remembers what they forgot."

Annabel was already grabbing her bag.

***

At the post office, the photo had been taped up next to the "lost cat" notices. A handwritten arrow in red pen pointed to it, beneath which someone had scrawled, *"Tragic."*

Outside the bakery, two women stood murmuring.

"She looks familiar, doesn't she?"

"Maybe from the market last year?"

"No, I think she was staying up by the woods. You know the one — the fancy rental with the glass porch."

***

In the Hare & Hound, the headshot had been pinned beside the dartboard.

Three people were sitting beneath it, not making eye contact.

Bernard was drying a mug that didn't need drying.

"Someone must know her," he muttered.

Annabel watched one woman — a visitor, maybe, or someone she hadn't noticed before — stare at the photo for a beat too long before picking up her drink and walking out.

Evie followed her with her eyes.

"Do we know her?"

"No," Annabel said. "But she knew *her*."

***

At the church noticeboard, someone had already started a note beneath the image:

"If you knew this girl or saw her recently, contact the local station."

Annabel added a small pin to hold it tighter.

***

By late afternoon, she had five people who claimed maybe they'd seen the girl.

Two of them clearly hadn't.

One might have.

And one — *the woman from the pub* — was now *unreachable*.

Evie raised an eyebrow as Annabel wrote her name in the notebook.

"You think she's running?"

Annabel shook her head.

"I think she thought no one would remember the girl's face.

And now that we do... she's not sure *what we'll remember next.*"

Chapter 9

Annabel had once said Little Firling was a village built on breadcrumbs.

Everyone leaves a trail—through the market, the green, the butcher's shop, the post office, the bakery or another place.

You just had to know where to look.

***

By noon, she had a map of the surrounding area spread across her kitchen table. A well-worn tourist brochure from the post office, annotated with *Evie's ferocious highlighter habit* and *Annabel's perfectly labelled pencil marks.*

"There are more rentals than I thought," Evie muttered. "Some of these barely look like they'd fit a suitcase."

"Doesn't take much space to disappear," Annabel said.

They focused on the ones *outside the village centre*—isolated homes, private retreats, long-stay cottages near the forest edge.

* * *

Annabel's first stop was the post office, where she asked about parcel pickups.

"People renting long-term usually collect their own mail, don't they?" she asked.

Mrs. Cuthbert blinked over her glasses. "Yes, dear, unless they're posh and send someone else."

"Has anyone new been in lately? Female, mid-thirties, quiet?"

"There was a woman who came in early Monday," she said. "Didn't say much. Bought stamps and a scratch card. Had a red scarf."

Annabel's pulse flickered.

"Do you know where she was staying?"

"Didn't say. But she was carrying a branded bag—Stonehill Lodge. Fancy place. You'd like the rhododendrons."

***

"People staying at Stonehill don't usually come in here," Bernard said at the Hare & Hound. "They're more wine cellar than ale tap, if you know what I mean."

But then he added:

"There was a woman. Quiet. Sat at the corner. Looked like she was trying not to be recognized. Red scarf, I think."

Evie leaned over her lemonade.

"That's the one from the boat, isn't it?"

Annabel nodded, slowly.

* * *

That evening, just before dusk, they took a walk up near the edge of the woods, where the road curved toward Stonehill Lodge.

It was set back behind hedges. Gated. The kind of place that *wanted to be left alone.*

But as they reached the bend, Annabel paused.

There—just past the hedge—*a figure.*

Red scarf.

Pulled tight.

Face half-turned.

The woman from the boat.

She moved toward the side entrance. Unlocked it. Slipped through.

Gone.

Evie let out a breath she didn't realize she'd been holding.

"She's staying there?"

"Or meeting someone," Annabel said. "Either way... *she came back.*"

Chapter 10

Stonehill Lodge sat at the edge of the woods like it had always belonged there — tall, quiet, and politely disinterested in the lives of everyone else.

But Annabel wasn't interested in its charm.

She was interested in *who had passed through its doors... and disappeared.*

***

The cottage's tourist registration logs were easy enough to access — the post office kept a list, as did the parish clerk.

“We like to know who’s staying where in case someone gets eaten by a badger,” Mrs. Cuthbert had said dryly.

But Stonehill Lodge was missing from the last two quarterly reports. No entry under its official name. No mention of bookings, staff changes, or maintenance calls.

“That’s odd,” Annabel said quietly, circling the blank space.

＊＊＊

Annabel checked with the local letting agency next.

“They handle the fancy stays,” Evie whispered as they walked through the high street. "Stonehill's always in their window."

Inside the office, the receptionist wore pastel pink and smiled like her teeth had never heard a lie.

"Oh, Stonehill Lodge," she said brightly.

"Booked all summer! Corporate retreats, mostly. Wellness types. Very exclusive."

"Do you know who was staying there in early July?" Annabel asked.

The receptionist blinked. "That's confidential."

Annabel smiled back. "Of course. But if someone went missing?"

"Then I'd suggest they *contact the police, officially.*"

* * *

Back outside, Annabel adjusted her bag and murmured:

"Too bright. Too fast. And lying through her teeth."

"You think she knows something?" Evie asked.

"I think she's been told not to say anything."

* * *

They looped back through the village, stopping by the grocer for milk. Annabel asked casually about deliveries up the hill.

"Big order went up there last week," the shop assistant said. "But the man who picked it up wasn't local. Had an accent. Northern. Drove a white van. Odd look about him."

"Was a woman with him?"

"Not that time. But the week before — yes. Red scarf. Quiet."

***

As the sun dropped low, they walked back to the bend near Stonehill Lodge.

The gate was still closed. The house still quiet.

"If she worked there before," Annabel said, "her name was scrubbed. And if she stayed there again... she was never supposed to be found."

Evie didn't answer.

Behind them, a car passed slowly — black, with tinted windows.

Neither of them looked until it was gone.

Chapter 11

The call came late in the day.

Annabel was in the garden, notebook open beside her, when her phone buzzed.

"Ms. Lennox Deighton? It's Layla Shaw — Dr. Jameson's assistant at the coroner's office. I understand that you have a keen interest in the body found in the water."

"Yes," Annabel said, already sitting up straighter.

"We re-examined the body. There's a tattoo — small, above the right ankle. Fully healed. Not recent — we're estimating a year, maybe two."

"What does it look like?"

"A wave, stylized. Tight spiral. Clean lines. Not decorative or trendy. More… symbolic."

"The ink?" she asked.

"Unusual. Not commercial-grade. Likely mixed privately — something you'd find in bespoke or commissioned work."

The photo arrived as soon as the call ended.

Annabel studied it. A wave, yes — but *closed in on itself.* Fluid. Deliberate. Like a secret only the skin was allowed to carry. "I've seen that before," she murmured.

***

She went inside, opened the drawer in her study — the one filled with things she never quite needed but could never throw away.

Old maps. A theatre program from five years ago. A postcard with no stamp.

And beneath it all — folded and tucked inside a faded leaflet from an estate tour — she found it.

"Virelai – A Retreat for Renewal"

The same *wave*. Curled on the cover like it was whispering.

Evie entered just as Annabel laid it on the table.

"What's that?"

"Her tattoo," Annabel said softly. "It's from this."

Evie leaned over the old tri-fold.

"For those who have survived, and are ready to live."

She blinked. "You think that's where she went?"

"I think that's where she was beginning."

✳✳✳

They searched.

Virelai's website was down. Their contact form bounced. Social media links redirected to blank accounts.

All that remained were cached blog posts from three or four years ago, waxing poetic about transformation and silence and sea air.

"Gone?" Evie said.

"Hidden," Annabel replied. "Or scrubbed."

***

She ran her finger over the symbol on the leaflet.

"She wasn't drifting. She made a choice. She started something."

A pause.

"Someone didn't want her to finish it."

Chapter 12

Stonehill Lodge stood as it always did — serene, secluded, and maddeningly silent behind its black iron gates. The gravel path that curved past the estate barely belonged to the village anymore. It belonged to time, and roots, and secrets.

"You're not really expecting her to walk nicely, are you?" Evie asked, as Persephone yanked her leash sideways with deliberate disdain.

"She's not on a walk," Annabel replied, calmly. "She's on patrol."

***

They weren't technically trespassing. Not yet. The lane that bordered the side garden of the Lodge was public — or at least unclaimed. And Annabel had every intention of keeping it that way... until Persephone darted toward a hedge and disappeared with all the subtlety of a grenade.

"Of course she did," Evie muttered, already diving after her.

Annabel followed the rustle and found Persephone crouched low beneath the thick ivy at the base of a stone wall — one paw scratching at something beneath the soil.

Not a mouse.

Not a bird.

Something plastic.

Annabel dropped to her knees.

"Oh," she said.

It was a bracelet.

Synthetic, dull green, caked in dirt. Cracked, but intact. A waterproof band — the kind given out at concerts, hospitals, or...

She turned it over.

There, stamped into the surface in faded white ink: *a spiral wave*.

***

Evie knelt beside her.

"Is that...?"

Annabel didn't answer. She was already pulling the Virelai leaflet from her bag.

She held the bracelet next to the printed logo.

Identical.

***

"That retreat wasn't just in Devon," she said softly.

"It was *here*."

A twig snapped.

They both turned.

At the edge of the trees — just beyond the hedge line — a figure stood watching them. Red scarf. Hair pulled back. Still.

The woman from the boat.

She didn't speak.

She didn't run.

She just looked at the bracelet in the hands of Annabel.

And then, slowly, turned and disappeared into the woods.

Chapter 13

The woman didn't come to them.

Annabel had to wait — sitting on the garden wall near Stonehill Lodge, Persephone curling around her feet like a silent guard. Evie stood a few paces off, pretending to scroll through her phone.

And then, finally, from the trees, the red scarf appeared again.

The woman didn't run this time.

***

"I don't know what you think I can give you," she said. Her voice was hoarse, her posture brittle. "I didn't hurt her."

Annabel nodded. "I don't think you did."

The woman's gaze lingered on the bracelet in the hands of Annabel — the one they'd unearthed with Persephone's stubborn claws.

"She buried that after Virelai," the woman said. "She told me she never wanted to look back. Only forward."

"But she called you," Annabel said gently. "Didn't she?"

The woman's jaw tightened. "Yes. A few weeks ago."

***

She sat down on the edge of the wall beside Annabel — not close, but not running anymore.

"She was excited. Nervous. Like… like she finally had something solid under her feet. Said she'd found people willing to help. Some of us. A few new ones."

"She wanted to build again. Not Virelai, exactly — something smaller. Local. Less structured. She had sketches. Vision boards. She wanted it to be art-based, this time. More… expressive."

Annabel exchanged a glance with Evie.

"Was there someone she worked on it with?"

The woman hesitated.

Then:

"Yes. Jules. He was... important to her. Not like that — at least, I don't think. But they were close. Came through Virelai the same time. She trusted him."

"Do you know his last name?"

"No. None of us used last names. It was part of the practice — you weren't your trauma, or your title. You were just... who you were."

"Do you know where he is?"

"I heard once that he opened a gallery. Something small. Somewhere near the coast. He talked about using his recovery to help others. That was always his dream."

A pause.

"If she trusted anyone with the truth, it was him."

***

Annabel stood, slowly.

The woman didn't move.

"If I find him," Annabel said softly, "what do I tell him?"

The red scarf fluttered slightly in the breeze.

"Tell him she was coming back.

And that she never stopped trying."

Chapter 14

It had taken most of the afternoon and several rounds of spiralling internet searches, but they'd finally found him.

"Jules – gallery owner, painter, advocate for emotional recovery through creative expression."

The gallery was called *The Still Current*, tucked along the winding lanes of a coastal town two hours from Little Firling. It had no flashy signage, just a hand-painted wooden placard and tall glass windows that let the light do most of the inviting.

Inside, the space was calm, like stepping into a memory someone had smoothed at the edges. The walls were covered in layered textures — waves and spirals, shattered pieces mended with gold, faces half-formed and reaching.

"This place breathes," Evie whispered.

Annabel said nothing but felt it too. It didn't scream gallery. It whispered sanctuary.

They weren't alone for long.

"Hi," said a man as he came out from a back room. "I'm Jules. Are you here for the exhibit or the workshop?"

He looked exactly as Annabel had imagined — tall, lean, a bit of charcoal smudged on his fingers, sleeves rolled back like he was always halfway through a thought.

"We were hoping to ask you about your work," Annabel said, offering a gentle smile.

"Of course," Jules replied. "I'm always happy to talk about art. It's what keeps me here, honestly."

* * *

They walked slowly through the gallery. Annabel stopped in front of a mixed-media piece: a single tree growing out of fractured stone, the roots cradling the cracks instead of breaking them.

"There's a lot of healing in these," she said.

"That's the idea," Jules replied. "I've always believed art helps people stitch themselves back together. Not neatly — but truthfully."

"Where did that belief come from?" she asked.

He hesitated. Not defensively — just thoughtfully.

"A retreat. Couple of years ago. We weren't names there. Just stories, broken and raw, learning how to breathe again."

As he spoke, he moved a canvas aside on the table, reaching for something — and his sleeve fell back.

****

There it was.

Encircling his wrist in quiet permanence — *the spiral wave.*

Not flashy. Not even coloured.

Just clean, soft lines. Etched like a vow.

Annabel's gaze flicked to it.

"Virelai?"

Jules froze. Looked down at his wrist. Then at her.

"I haven't heard that name in a long time."

He rubbed the tattoo lightly with his thumb, like it still grounded him.

"It's where I found art again. Where I found... myself, I suppose."

"You wear it on your wrist," Annabel noted.

He gave a small smile. "So, I see it every time I paint."

Chapter 15

Jules has mentioned that Virelai had never been big.

Not flashy. Not corporate. Not the kind of retreat that landed on wellness blogs with crisp drone footage and detox testimonials.

It had been small. Intentional. Quietly powerful.

And it was gone.

***

Annabel sat at her desk, the afternoon light slanting through the curtains. Persephone was curled in a beam of sun, tail twitching like she too felt something stirring in the air.

On her screen were old webpages, archived blog posts, cached interviews. Most links were dead. The ones that remained were soft and strange — phrases like *"emotional recalibration,"* *"trauma untangled," "healing in stillness."*

"No board of directors," Evie said, peering over her shoulder. "No PR. No big social media footprint."

"No accident," Annabel murmured.

***

They had contacted one of the Virelai staff listed in a guest blog from four years ago — a woman named Mara Sanderson, who now worked with a seaside grief recovery centre.

She'd been hesitant to talk at first.

But when Annabel mentioned the bracelet... and the girl found in the water... she agreed to meet them. Quietly. Discreetly.

***

Mara was older than Annabel had expected. Late fifties, with hair cropped short and silver at the edges. She met them in a garden café, her fingers wrapped tight around her teacup as if it grounded her.

"Virelai was never supposed to grow big," she said. "That was the point. We wanted people to come and unspool. No pressure. No performances. Not selling your healing to anyone."

"Why did it close?" Annabel asked.

A pause.

Mara's mouth twisted. "Funding. Or the disappearance of it."

"There was a backer?"

"Yes. Quiet. Generous. No one knew who they were — only two or three core members ever met them. They wanted anonymity. Said the work mattered more than the name."

"And one day...?"

"One day the money vanished. Bookings stopped. Emails bounced. The house was sold quietly. No explanation. Just... gone."

∗∗∗

Evie frowned. "Do you think someone *wanted* it to close?"

Mara hesitated.

Then:

"I think someone didn't like who it was helping. Or who was starting to heal."

"That's a strange thing to be afraid of."

Mara looked at them, sharp and sad.

"You'd be surprised how threatened some people feel when someone learns how to live without them."

Chapter 16

Jules didn't remember the exact moment Virelai closed — not like a door slamming, but like a breeze that simply stopped moving.

One week, the messages slowed.

The next, the bookings vanished.

And by the time he'd emailed Mara — the retreat coordinator — the site was gone. Just... gone.

"They said funding dried up," Jules told Annabel, eyes distant. "No warning. No apology. Just: 'We're unable to accommodate your request at this time.' That was it."

They sat in the back room of his gallery, surrounded by paint-stained aprons and unfinished canvases. Annabel said nothing, letting him work through the pieces on his own.

"I thought it was just bad luck. A small operation losing money. But Em, a friend I met at Virelai,…"

He stopped.

"She didn't think it was an accident, did she?" Annabel said gently.

Jules exhaled.

"She was quiet about it, but… yes. Something changed in her."

"She seems someone that make quite an impression on you. Please tell me more about her," said Annabel.

***

Jules has said that she had been so alive after Virelai — still fragile, still rebuilding, but *hopeful.*

She talked about starting her own version. Smaller. Looser. Less rules, more soul.

They met once every two months — short visits, quick coffees, long messages.

"I remember she stopped showing up with her sketchbook," Jules said. "She said it made her feel exposed. Like someone might see it."

Annabel leaned forward. "Did she mention anyone from her past?"

"Not by name. But she said, once—" he paused, searching for the exact words.

"She said, 'He found me. Or maybe he never stopped looking.'"

***

"Who was he?"

"I don't know. But she changed after that. She stopped planning. She got restless. One time I showed her a flyer for an artists' co-op… she just stared at it and said, 'I don't get to have that.'"

Jules stood up suddenly, walking to the window.

"There was a man," Jules said after a pause. "Tall. Wore grey. He came to the gallery once. Didn't buy anything. Didn't speak to me."

"But when Emily came in a few days later, she saw him. She froze. Said she needed to leave."

"I asked if she knew him. She said, 'He thinks I'm his. And he doesn't like when I say no.'"

He ran a hand through his hair.

"She said he had money. Connections. That he always got what he wanted. That people listened to him. Did things for him."

"She'd found out what he was capable of. And she was scared."

***

Annabel's voice was low. "Did she ever say his name?"

"No," Jules said, slowly. "She said she didn't want to speak it. That saying it kept him alive in her head. That forgetting him... was the only thing that made her feel free."

Chapter 17

It was the only clue they had — *Ella March* — a name Jules had mentioned quietly, like a confession.

He'd seen it once, scribbled in the corner of an envelope Emily had left behind during a visit to the gallery.

"She never said it out loud," he'd told them. *"But she was different that day. Jittery. Focused. Like she was preparing to be someone else."*

Annabel hadn't asked more. She didn't need to. If Emily had used a new name, she'd done it for protection.

Now that name had led them here.

***

The rental agency confirmed it: Ella March had booked a small cottage just outside the village. One month. Cash up front. No emergency contact. No ID check. Just a quiet let and a note that the tenant had left suddenly and never returned.

The door was unlocked when they arrived.

***

Inside, the air felt still — not forgotten, but *interrupted*.

Like someone had left in the middle of breathing.

A canvas leaned in the corner, half-covered with a cloth. A jar of brushes rested beside a chipped porcelain mug. On the wall, a corkboard held just one pinned scrap: *a sketched tree, its roots tangled around a spiral wave.*

"She didn't pack," Evie murmured. "She didn't plan to leave."

Annabel crossed to the canvas and lifted the cloth.

Underneath, a painting — unfinished, raw. A woman at the edge of a cliff, arms lifted toward a churning sea.

On the windowsill sat a small box. Inside, a few notecards with quotes:

"The self is not a fixed point. It's a tide, always shifting."

"Healing is resistance."

"What we rebuild can never be taken again."

Annabel closed the lid gently. "She was still building," she said. "Until someone stopped her."

✳✳✳

They met the woman in the red scarf again at a quiet teahouse, on the edge of the village.

"Ella March?" she repeated. "That wasn't the name she used at Virelai, but that's her writing."

"We need to understand what happened to the retreat," Annabel said. "Who pulled the strings."

The woman hesitated, then sighed.

"You need to speak to Arlo Lancaster, the founder of Virelai."

***

It took three calls and the name of an old mutual friend to get a meeting.

Arlo lived in a converted boathouse — the kind that looked like it had been beautiful once. When he opened the door, he looked like a man who had *once created something sacred... and watched it vanish.*

When Annabel asked what happened to Virelai, Arlo didn't even sit down.

"Staff left. Not because they wanted to — because they were *poached.*

Food deliveries delayed. Orders mysteriously cancelled.

Other retreats opened up with our programs. Our language. Our methods. *Cheaper. Flashier."*

He shook his head.

"People say it was money. No. It was *pressure.* Someone didn't like what we were doing.

And *they made it harder and harder to exist."*

***

"Did you know who was behind it?"

"No," Arlo said. "But there was one moment I won't forget."

"Someone asked for a guest record to be scrubbed. No name. Just an anonymous request.

Legal-sounding. A 'privacy concern.'

I said no.

A week later... *the funding vanished.*"

He looked at the sketch Annabel had placed on the table.

"And that?" he said, voice soft. "That was hers. She was the one they wanted gone."

Chapter 18

The gallery was quiet when Annabel returned.

Jules was standing at a canvas, brush in hand, the colours frozen mid-thought.

He didn't turn when the bell chimed.

Annabel stepped in, slowly.

"I have something to tell you," she said gently.

He paused. Lowered the brush.

"It's about Em, isn't it?"

She nodded once.

A pause.

"She was found. In the water, near Little Firling."

The brush in his hand tilted.

"Found," he repeated. "But is she okay?"

Annabel looked at him — really looked. The flicker of hope. The held breath.

She shook her head.

"She's gone, Jules. I'm sorry."

"I was scared to ask why you were asking about Em before."

***

He turned his face slightly, as if light might break him. Then placed the brush down with quiet precision.

"She was trying to come back," he said, almost to himself. "She had so much left."

"I spoke to Arlo Lancaster," Annabel said.

Jules paused. Then nodded. "And?"

"He confirmed what we thought. Virelai didn't collapse. *It was sabotaged.* From the inside out."

Still, Jules didn't speak. He dabbed blue into the corner of the canvas — too dark for sky, too light for sea.

Annabel stepped closer.

"And they were after her."

Jules let the brush fall into a jar of murky water.

"She always knew," he said quietly. "She just didn't say it."

He moved to the back table, where a small stack of cards lay — sketches, quote cuttings, pages from a journal she'd once given him to read.

He picked up the top one and held it out to Annabel.

In careful writing:

"To be known is the most dangerous kind of freedom."

***

"I need her full name," Annabel said softly. "To find out what else he took from her."

Jules was quiet for a long time.

Then:

"She told it to me the day Virelai closed. Said she was tired of hiding.

She said it like it was a confession — and a promise."

He looked at Annabel.

"Emily Joiner. That was her name."

***

Outside, the light was beginning to soften. Shadows stretched long and slow across the cobbled street.

Inside the gallery, Jules stood still.

"I called her Em for so long," he said. "It never occurred to me that someone could want to silence *Emily*."

Annabel stepped forward; her voice low.

"Someone did. And now I'm going to find out who."

Chapter 19

It was an old email. Arlo had almost deleted it a dozen times over the years.

But now, after his conversation with Annabel, he read it again — slowly, deliberately — this time with anger he'd buried long ago. The signature still stood out at the bottom of the legal notice:

Harlan Voss, on behalf of Vesden Private Holdings Ltd.

He remembered the unease. The way the funding vanished overnight. The feeling that someone had not just backed out — but *deliberately erased something important.*

So, he forwarded the email to Annabel with one sentence:

"Here's your ghost."

***

Annabel stared at the name on the screen. "Harlan Voss."

Evie frowned. "Never heard of him."

"Because he doesn't want to be heard of," Annabel murmured. "That's the point."

They dug in.

Within an hour, they'd found the shell company — Vesden Private Holdings — a quiet owner of multiple wellness properties, all of which had closed quietly, one by one, within a year of Virelai's shutdown.

Each one had focused on recovery, transformation, healing. Each had been popular with survivors, trauma therapists, or spiritual counsellors.

And each had been silenced.

"It's like someone bought up every space where people went to reclaim themselves," Evie said. "And then locked the doors."

"Not someone," Annabel said. "Harlan Voss."

***

The phone rang.

It was the coroner.

"We've completed toxicology," he said. "Trace amounts of a benzodiazepine in the victim's bloodstream. Not lethal, but enough to cause disorientation or unconsciousness."

"No alcohol?"

"None."

"And the lungs?"

"Definitely chlorinated water. Pool water."

A pause.

"She didn't drown by accident," the coroner said quietly. "Someone made sure of it."

***

That evening, they stopped into the Hare & Hound — not to chase leads, but because they needed tea, and something warm, and the company of a place that didn't lie.

Bernard was polishing glasses behind the bar. Henry Griggs, the barkeeper, leaned on a stool near the window, watching the sun sink behind the hills.

"Oddest thing last month," Henry said suddenly, pointing his mug in the air. "That black car. Sleek thing. Looked like a spaceship trying to blend in with sheep."

Annabel turned.

"Black car?"

"Maserati, maybe?" Bernard offered. "Definitely foreign. Parked up by the pay station. Long time too — must've overstayed."

"No one ever figured out who it belonged to," Henry added. "Didn't match anyone staying at the Lodge."

"Didn't match anyone at all," Bernard said.

Evie looked at Annabel, her brow furrowed.

Annabel didn't answer immediately.

Instead, she stared at the firelight dancing in her tea, then quietly said,

"If that car wasn't here for the village..."

A pause. Heavy. Real.

"Then we need to find out *who* it was here for."

Chapter 20

Annabel had always believed in silence. The kind that carried truth—not the absence of sound, but the pause before someone said the thing that mattered most.

This silence, though?

It was the silence of things being *carefully hidden.*

Until now.

***

The next morning, Annabel was halfway through composing a carefully worded request to the council when Evie walked in, holding two mugs of tea and a raised brow.

"You're trying to get parking records?"

Annabel nodded. "They issued a fine to a black Maserati the same day Emily disappeared. I need to know who it was registered to."

Evie set down the tea and pulled out her phone.

"You know my cousin Andy works admin at County Traffic, right? He's not a rule-breaker, but... let's say he appreciates context."

Ten minutes and one very polite phone call later, Evie glanced up and smiled.

"Check your email."

The document was there — plain, official, and damning.

License Plate: HX11 VSS

Issued To: *Harlan Voss*

Registered Address: London — private estate

Annabel exhaled slowly. "There he is."

"We've got a car. We've got a name. And now..." she tapped the screen, "we've got him parked *right here* the day she vanished."

***

The Hare & Hound was quiet again that afternoon.

This time, Annabel didn't come for tea. She came to ask questions.

Bernard was at the bar. Ronnie Parkes, the postman, leaned near the window with a crossword puzzle and a pint.

"You remember that Maserati?" she asked.

Bernard nodded. "Hard to forget. Sleek. Arrogant. Didn't belong."

Ronnie piped in. "Saw it swing in just after noon that day. I was doing deliveries. Parked clean. Rich people always park like they're being watched."

"Did you see who was driving it?"

Ronnie squinted. "Tall man. Grey suit. Hair slicked. Didn't say much.

Didn't even go to the pub. Walked toward the sea."

Annabel's voice was steady.

"Alone?"

"Went in alone," Ronnie said. "Can't say how he came out."

***

Back at Honeystone Cottage, Annabel sat with the parking citation spread out next to a notebook full of fragments. Timelines. Names. Half-finished quotes.

She drew a simple line from the *name* *"Harlan Voss"* to the *Vesden's Holding that owned a villa along the coast.*

She paused.

Then drew another line — *from the villa... to the date of Emily's disappearance.*

The triangle was complete.

***

"He came here to be unseen," she said aloud.

"But he left just enough behind."

Chapter 21

"I've been digging into Vesden's holdings," Annabel said, scrolling on her tablet as they walked. "Most of it's buried under trusts and subsidiaries, but there's one property that stands out."

"Because it's big?" Evie asked.

"Because it's quiet. No public listings, no guest records, no staff—except a private management firm. And it's here."

She pointed to the map on screen. The marker glowed just above the coastal road.

"Less than three minutes from where the Maserati was parked."

"You think it's his?" Evie asked.

"It's not listed under his name," Annabel said. "But the holding company matches the one that backed out of Virelai. Same legal representative. Same mailing address. It's him."

The sea was calm when they arrived — too calm.

The villa sat just off the coastal road, set back enough to be private, but not hidden. It wasn't grand or glamorous; in fact, it looked like a place that had *paid to look ordinary*. Low-key landscaping, minimalist lines, whitewashed walls. Just enough silence to feel curated.

"This is it?" Evie asked. "Doesn't look like a murder scene."

"That's the point," Annabel said. "Perhaps it was never meant to be."

***

They stood at the edge of the private driveway. The gate was closed, but the villa, owned by the rental company of Harlan Voss was currently unoccupied. The management company had listed it quietly for short-term lets — and as it happened, Annabel had called ahead.

A man named Peter from the management firm met them at the gate. Clipboard. Keys. Corporate smile.

"Bit unusual," he said as they walked up the drive. "But we're always happy to accommodate—"

"It was booked under the Vesden umbrella," Annabel said casually. "You've handled it for a while?"

Peter blinked. "Uh, not personally. But yes. High-end client. Privacy contracts. We don't get many details."

"We're not looking for details," Annabel replied. "Just impressions."

He opened the door and waved them inside.

"I'll be on the porch if you need anything."

***

The villa was too clean.

Not spotless — just too perfectly arranged. The kind of clean that came *after something.*

Evie ran a finger along the edge of the marble island. "This place feels like it's been exhaled."

Annabel moved quietly. Through the open-plan kitchen, into the master bedroom. The air had a faint, metallic coolness to it. And under it, something else.

Chlorine.

She knelt beside the sliding glass doors that led out to the private pool. Pressed her fingers to the base of the handle. It clicked open with a soft snick.

Outside, the pool glistened. Empty. Blue as an alibi.

"You think it happened here?" Evie asked.

"I think she never left this place alive."

* * *

Inside, they checked the bedroom closets. One was empty. The other held a single hanger — the kind used for a dress. Plastic, thin, slightly bent.

Evie picked up something from the corner of the vanity: a tiny pearl earring.

"Do you think it's hers?"

"If it's not, he left more ghosts than just Emily."

＊

Back outside, the pool was still. Blue. Serene.

It didn't belong to a crime scene. But Annabel didn't trust peace that came in silence.

She knelt by the edge and dipped a small glass vial into the water, sealing it tight.

Evie stood behind her. "Think it'll match what was in her lungs?"

"I don't want to think it," Annabel said. "I want to *prove* it."

Evie glanced back at the house. "You really think this is where she died?"

Annabel capped the vial.

"I think this is where someone made sure she'd never speak again."

*　*　*

Evie stood at the edge of the pool, watching the sunlight ripple against the surface.

"You think he planned to drown her here?"

Annabel shook her head.

"I don't think that was the plan."

She held the vial of water a little tighter.

"I think he brought her here to win her back. One last time. On his terms."

"And when she didn't break—he did."

Chapter 22

The next morning brought fog. The kind that crawled over windows and made everything feel like a secret trying to hide itself again.

Annabel stood at the kitchen counter, watching her tea steep, when her phone buzzed.

It was PC Tom Oakes.

"Preliminary report just came in," he said. "From the pool sample you handed off."

"Anything?"

"You were right," he said. "The chlorine levels, trace diatoms—it's practically identical to the water found in her lungs."

"So?"

"It was the crime scene, Annabel. No doubt."

***

She closed her eyes for half a second. "Thank you."

"There's more. I've flagged the name — Harlan Voss — with traffic surveillance teams. The reg plate from the parking ticket matches a vehicle that passed through the Kingsbridge toll camera three days before she was found. Face isn't clear yet... but we'll get it."

"Do you think he knows we're close?"

"If he's smart, he'll already be in another country. If he's arrogant…"

"He'll be watching," she finished.

***

At Honeystone Cottage, Evie had taken over half the dining room. Paperwork, post-it notes, and her laptop charger tangled around coffee mugs like ivy.

"This guy. He's good," she muttered. "Built an entire shadow structure and nobody ever bothered to check who was behind the curtain."

Annabel joined her.

"Because he knew where to hide. In silence. In paperwork."

Evie clicked through property filings. "Vesden Holdings owns five properties. One in Little Firling. One in Surrey. One in Florence—show-off—and..."

She paused.

"This. One of the founding companies on an old deed—it's not a business. It's two initials. S.H."

Annabel frowned. "That's something."

"It gets better," Evie said. "He didn't use 'Vesden' on that filing. He used a shell firm: *Harns Advisory Ltd.*"

Annabel blinked. The name pulled at something.

"Harns?"

"Random, right?"

Annabel pulled a notepad toward her and scribbled:

Harlan Voss

She stared at the letters. Rearranged them with tiles. Frowned.

"There's something inside this," she said. "I just can't—"

A sudden, soft *thump*.

Persephone landed lightly on the table and immediately inserted herself into the puzzle. With one paw, she shifted two of the letter tiles Annabel had laid out — pushing them apart — and then, with a delicate claw tap, nudged one into the centre.

Evie stared.

"Did she just—"

Annabel's eyes locked on the rearranged letters.

H–A–R–N–S

Right there.

She whispered:

"Harns."

Then, quietly, like unlocking a door:

"Salvo."

"Salvo Harns."

Persephone sat down, tail flicking once like a final keystroke.

Annabel looked at her. "You always knew."

***

Outside, the fog had started to lift.

But inside, the name sat between them like something *still breathing.*

"If that's his real name," Evie whispered, "we can find him."

"No," Annabel said.

"Now, we will."

Chapter 23

It started with a donation receipt.

Buried in a bundle of public records Annabel had requested through a backchannel—small grant files, retreat donations, wellness funders—there was a familiar name.

Harns Advisory Ltd.

Listed as a *silent donor* to a now-defunct private wellness foundation in Surrey.

Evie hovered behind her, reading over her shoulder.

"Wellness through structure," she read aloud from the mission statement.

"God. That sounds clinical enough to be sinister."

Annabel nodded. "It shut down two years before Virelai. No scandals. Just… vanished. Quietly."

"And he was behind it?"

"Harns was listed as an advisory contact," Annabel said. "No face. Just a name."

But names, now, were enough.

∗∗∗

From there, they traced more.

Three shell companies

Two advisory roles on holistic therapy centres that had shuttered

A retreat in Provence, sold to developers after the founder mysteriously pulled out

Each one had been described the same way:

Promising. Safe. Life-changing.

Until the silence.

Until the money left.

***

Evie clicked through another document.

"He didn't just fund retreats. He shut them down. Quietly. One after another."

Annabel tapped the page.

"It's like he was dismantling places that gave people strength. Quietly removing safe spaces."

Evie scrolled again. "He didn't need to be visible to be dangerous."

"Exactly," Annabel said. "And if Emily knew how he was... she might've known what he was capable of."

A pause.

"Maybe she'd seen him do it before."

Evie clicked open another document.

"And he used healing to do it."

She tilted the laptop so Annabel could see.

A photo. A low-res, unsmiling man in the background of a retreat launch event, standing behind a row of smiling board members.

"That him?" Evie asked.

"Yes." Annabel didn't hesitate.

"He made sure his name was quiet. His photo quieter. But he couldn't vanish entirely."

***

Then came a whisper from a place they hadn't expected.

Simon Deane called.

Annabel and Evie met Simon while investigating what happened to a young actress 20 years ago. He had contacts in financial circles and was able to secure the funds for a play then.

"You said the name was Salvo Harns?" Simon asked, his voice unusually careful.

"Yes. Do you know him?"

"Only by reputation. The kind of man who funds things to own them. I saw his name once—quiet donation to a publishing collective I used to be part of. Three months later, they went under."

A pause.

"I think he enjoys the power of letting people believe they're safe. Then proving they never were."

***

That night, Annabel stared out the window as the wind teased the lavender bushes along the back wall of the garden.

Salvo Harns wasn't a ghost anymore.

He was a man.

With land. With money. With a trail.

And *she had him. No more a ghost.*

Chapter 24

The rain was soft that afternoon, barely more than mist. Honeystone Cottage glowed golden under its lamps, but inside, everything had gone still.

Jules sat on the edge of the armchair, twisting a teacup between his hands.

"I keep thinking about something she said."

Annabel and Evie waited.

"It was just after one of the group sessions at Virelai. She didn't talk much, not then. But we were walking by the lake and she said—"

"*It always disappears when I finally start to feel safe.*"

Evie sat forward. "She meant?"

Jules shrugged. "She didn't explain. But the way she said it—it wasn't about people. It was about places. Retreats. Spaces."

He hesitated.

"She told me once she'd been somewhere in France. Not for long. Said it helped, for a little while. But then the funding pulled out, and everything shut down overnight."

A silence settled between them. The sound of rain tapping gently on the kitchen window.

Annabel opened her notebook. "Did she ever mention who funded it?"

"No names. Just that it always ended the same way. Like someone didn't want her to get better."

* * *

Later, over a quiet dinner, the pieces sat between them on the table like puzzle fragments soaked in wine and shadows.

"He didn't just kill her," Evie whispered. "He *chased her healing* and took that too."

Annabel nodded. "Because if she healed, she could walk away from him."

"And he couldn't let that happen."

* * *

It was nearly midnight when Annabel's phone buzzed again.

It was PC Tom Oakes.

"We might have something," he said, voice low. "There's a property registered under Salvo Harns. Not in his main holdings, but a personal purchase. Quiet. Remote."

Annabel stood. "Where?"

"Scotland. A lodge near the coast. Rented under another shell company, but the payment trail leads back to him. He's there."

"How long?"

"Maybe three days. Maybe longer."

"You think that he knows we're closing in?"

"I think he's waiting."

***

Annabel walked to the window. The rain had stopped, but the air still felt heavy. Charged.

"He ran when she said no," she said quietly.

"But this time... we're the ones coming for him."

Chapter 25

The cliffs near the coast stood quiet and wind-scoured, the sea humming below like a secret held too long. A narrow lay-by just off the main road, scrubby trees leaning inland from years of storms, a rusted bin chained to a post.

"He stopped here," Tom said, checking the log on his clipboard. "Twelve minutes. No traffic cams nearby. Too remote."

"Too perfect," Annabel muttered.

Evie was already scanning the area, glancing at the edge of the trees, then back at the overgrown ditch running behind the bin.

It was Persephone who made the first sound — a low growl, ears flattening.

"She's got something," Evie said.

They found it buried under layers of old bin bags and sand — wrapped in what looked like an old hoodie, shoved into a torn canvas tote.

A faint flash of blue.

A phone.

＊

It was water-damaged but not destroyed.

The SIM was gone.

The screen had a single, jagged crack.

But the device was whole.

Evie held it carefully in her hands. "This is it."

"If she had auto-sync turned on..." Annabel said softly.

Tom pulled out his phone and flicked on his mobile hotspot.

"Let's give her signal."

They waited.

Then—

BZZZ

A flicker. A buzz. A sync icon.

And then it started:

A *location history* dot — the villa.

A *calendar entry*: "Meeting H.V."

A *photo* — a shot of the pool, slightly tilted, taken from behind a glass door.

Evie's thumb hovered over the screen.

"It's a photo of the pool."

Tom frowned. "Why would she—?"

Annabel stepped closer.

"Because she knew."

"Not everything. Not yet. But enough. Just enough to be afraid."

She pointed at the angle of the image.

"It's not framed like a memory. It's *a message.*"

A pause.

"She was telling us where to look."

And finally—

A drafted, unsent message:

"If I don't come back, his name is—"

It cut off. But it was enough.

***

Annabel stared at the screen.

"She tried to tell us."

Evie looked away, blinking fast. "She did."

***

That night, back at Honeystone, the phone sat between them like a beacon.

And outside, the wind changed.

Salvo Harns had erased places, voices, even memories.

But this?

He forgot that *data remembers*.

Chapter 26

The clouds over Scotland rolled low and heavy, bruised with coming rain. The lodge stood in the middle of nowhere — just stone, sea, and silence.

Annabel stepped out of the car with Tom Oakes beside her. It has been a long journey from Little Firling. The wind whipped across the gravel, and Persephone, curled in her travel crate, let out a soft growl like she knew what was coming.

Inside the car behind them, another officer checked his weapon.

"He's still in there?" Annabel asked quietly.

Tom nodded. "Local surveillance says yes. He's alone. No signs of movement since last night."

"He knows we're coming."

"He's probably been watching every step."

***

They didn't storm the lodge. Not yet.

Instead, Tom approached the front slowly, one hand raised, his badge clipped to his coat. Annabel stayed back, watching through binoculars as the curtains inside shifted — just once.

A shadow moved.

Then nothing.

"He's stalling," Annabel said. "He's thinking."

"Good," Tom said into his communication device. "Let him panic."

✳✳✳

The entry team moved in ten minutes later. Quiet. Coordinated.

A knock.

A wait.

Another knock.

Then: *CRACK* — the door opened fast, too fast.

Salvo Harns stood in the doorway, perfectly still.

He was dressed like a man about to go sailing: boat shoes, cable-knit sweater, sunglasses tucked into his collar. Completely composed.

"This is ridiculous," he said before anyone spoke.

"You have no evidence. No warrant."

Tom held out the printed warrant. "We do. Actually, we have both."

"And I'll have a barrister within the hour."

"That won't change what the phone says," Annabel replied.

"I don't own a phone."

"Not yours," she said calmly. "Emily's."

His jaw ticked. Just once.

“I don’t know an Emily.”

“Oh, yes,” Annabel said. “You do.”

***

Inside, everything was clean. Gleaming. Ordered.

But it wasn’t the kind of order that came from peace.

It wasn’t the kind that follows guilt.

It came from *power.*

From the *need to dominate every surface.*

The kind of order that says:

“Nothing happened here. Because I say so.”

They didn't find anything immediately incriminating.

But Tom didn't care.

"We don't need what's in here," he said. "We've got what was out there."

***

Back in the car, Annabel watched Salvo through the rear window as he sat handcuffed, saying nothing.

"He doesn't look nervous," Evie whispered.

"He isn't," Annabel said. "Because he thinks he'll talk his way out."

A pause.

"But we don't need him to speak."

"We have Emily now."

Chapter 27

The headlines exploded before breakfast.

"Financier of Silence: Salvo Harns Arrested in Connection with Drowning Death."

"Beneath the Surface: Private Wellness Mogul Investigated for More."

"Whispers in Retreats: Who Did Salvo Harns Fund — and Who Did He Silence?"

Annabel scrolled slowly through the screen, her tea going cold. The photos were clinical — his mugshot, the lodge, a satellite image of the villa. But the commentary?

That was fire.

"They're tearing him apart," Evie said, standing over her shoulder.

"He's not the story anymore," Annabel replied. "The *network* is."

***

The phone didn't stop ringing for two days.

Journalists. Former retreat attendees. Anonymous callers.

A *whistleblower from Vesden Holdings.*

A *former therapist from one of the dismantled wellness centres.*

"He used emotional leverage," one email read. "Charmed donors.

Controlled founders. Then buried the ones who got too loud."

Another message was darker. Shorter.

"I think he did it before. Not just to her."

***

Tom Oakes dropped by late in the evening with an update.

"The Crown Prosecution Services are moving fast. We've got the digital trail. The cloud data. Phone location. Eyewitnesses. And now this…"

He handed Annabel a document.

A sealed case file from France.

A retreat shutdown.

A young woman vanished.

Ruled suicide.

No body found.

Funding pulled three weeks after she disappeared.

"And guess who backed that retreat through a now-dissolved shell?"

Evie's hand flew to her mouth.

Annabel didn't flinch.

"He's been doing this longer than we thought."

✳✳✳

Outside, a storm began. Not just in the sky — but in the world Salvo Harns used to own.

He had ruled through silence.

Now, *his silence was a scream.*

And people were *finally listening.*

Chapter 28

The courtroom was cold.

Not from the air — the temperature was fine — but from the walls, the silence, the sheer restraint of it all. Order, formality. A theatre of facts.

Salvo Harns sat like a statue at the defence table, flanked by two solicitors and dressed in a suit that probably cost more than most people made in a month. His expression never wavered.

Blank.

Controlled.

Composed.

Annabel sat in the gallery, a notebook in her lap, Persephone quietly curled at her feet like the judgment of ancient gods.

She hadn't planned to be here. But when the Crown Prosecution listed the evidence — when they showed *the pool photo Emily had taken*, when they read aloud the *unsent message on her phone*, when they confirmed the *GPS logs and the dumped phone's recovery*...

She knew she had to see it through.

✳✳✳

Evie leaned in. "Do you think he'll speak?"

"Only if he thinks he can win."

***

The trial moved with precision. Testimonies were clinical.

Jules spoke quietly, but with steady eyes.

"She wanted to rebuild something. After what he took from her."

Tom Oakes presented the timeline. The forensics. The digital footprint that tethered Emily to her killer like a red thread no lawyer could cut.

And then, the audio logs.

Emily's voice, faint but clear, reading a journal entry saved to her cloud account weeks before her death.

"I've started to feel like myself again. Like I don't belong to anyone."

The courtroom didn't make a sound.

Salvo didn't blink.

***

The verdict didn't come that day. Of course not.

But it didn't have to.

Because outside the courthouse, in the sea of reporters and bystanders, *people already knew.*

Emily wasn't just a name anymore.

She was *a storm.*

A signal that survived.

A life that refused to disappear quietly.

And Salvo?

He no longer looked like a man in control.

He looked like a man *waiting for the echo of a name he buried to finally destroy him.*

Epilogue

Honeystone Cottage smelled faintly of rosemary and rain.

The garden, still damp from the morning shower, glowed under a soft sun, the roses heavy with droplets and the dahlias finally uncurling into full bloom. The village was quiet — the kind of quiet that felt earned, not uneasy.

Inside, Persephone lay stretched across the kitchen windowsill, one paw twitching in her sleep. Annabel leaned against the counter, a steaming cup of tea in her hands, while Evie flipped through the newspaper at the table.

"Front page," she murmured. "He's everywhere."

"And nowhere now," Annabel replied.

They sat in easy silence for a moment, the kind that didn't need to fill space. Not anymore.

"I keep thinking about Emily," Evie said.

"So do I."

A pause.

"Do you think she knew?" Evie asked. "That someone would find her story. Finish it."

Annabel looked out the window, toward the garden. The wind brushed past the lavender, and somewhere in the hedge, a wren chirped once before falling quiet again.

"Maybe not," she said. "But I think... she left enough of herself behind to make sure we could."

***

Later, as the sun began to drift lower in the sky, Persephone stirred and padded over to Annabel's lap, curling up without ceremony.

Evie looked up from her notebook, eyebrows raised.

"You're going to rest now, right?"

Annabel smiled faintly, stroking Persephone's ears.

"Eventually."

Evie smirked. "You say that every time."

Annabel didn't answer. She just looked down at the envelope in her lap — thick paper, hand-addressed, no return sender.

She hadn't opened it yet.

But the words on the front were familiar.

"To the one who notices everything."

About the Author

Belinda writes layered mysteries where memory lingers, landscapes remember, and silence speaks louder than words. Her stories slip between the literary and the intimate—part atmospheric suspense, part quiet reckoning. Rooted in a love for islands, history, and hidden truths, her work invites readers to linger in the in-between.

She believes some lands carry echoes of everything they've witnessed—grief, joy, betrayal—and that nostalgia for a place is its own kind of story.

She also writes heartfelt children's stories that whisper courage into quiet hearts. With magical ladybugs, story-saving oaks, and brave little girls like Maia, Belinda hopes to help young readers find their own voice—and use it boldly.

When she's not writing, Belinda tends to her garden, guided by the rustle of leaves, the smell of earth, and the quiet company of two cats who always seem to know more than they let on.

www.ingramcontent.com/pod-product-compliance
Lightning Source LLC
Chambersburg PA
CBHW031536310726
48971CB00008B/2498